Stray Birds

漂鳥集

泰戈爾　著
糜文開　譯

國家圖書館出版品預行編目資料

漂鳥集 / 泰戈爾著, 糜文開譯. －－初版二刷. －－臺北市:
三民, 2019
　　面；　公分. －－(世界文學)
　　ISBN 978－957－14－6403－9 （平裝）
　1. 印度文學 2. 詩

867.51　　　　　　　　　　　　　　　　　107005406

© 漂 鳥 集

著 作 人	泰戈爾
譯 者	糜文開
責任編輯	陳怡安
美術設計	蔡季吟
插畫設計	蔡瓅葳
發 行 人	劉振強
著作財產權人	三民書局股份有限公司
發 行 所	三民書局股份有限公司
	地址　臺北市復興北路386號
	電話　(02)25006600
	郵撥帳號　0009998－5
門 市 部	(復北店)臺北市復興北路386號
	(重南店)臺北市重慶南路一段61號
出版日期	初版一刷　2018年9月
	初版二刷　2019年6月
編 號	S 870130

行政院新聞局登記證局版臺業字第○二○○號

有著作權‧不准侵害

ISBN　978－957－14－6403－9　（平裝）

http://www.sanmin.com.tw　三民網路書店
※本書如有缺頁、破損或裝訂錯誤，請寄回本公司更換。

泰戈爾在臺灣的代言人：糜文開

　　印度，有點熟悉又遙遠神祕的國度。古遠的天竺故事和印度歌舞人人皆有印象，但印度現代的歷史和文學卻又似乎相當陌生。泰戈爾可能是大家最容易想到的現代印度作家了：身為亞洲首位獲得諾貝爾文學獎的詩人，泰戈爾在二十世紀前半的中國名聲響亮，不但曾親訪中國，與徐志摩、林徽因的交往讓人津津樂道，梁啟超也為他取了個中文名字「竺震旦」。鄭振鐸在 1922 年譯出了他的《飛鳥集》，更是傳頌一時。

　　但在戰後的臺灣，五四詩人已遠，《飛鳥集》因鄭振鐸「附匪」而名列禁書書單，泰戈爾的名聲仍得以維持不墜，必須歸功於糜文開。臺灣市面上雖

能見到鄭振鐸的《飛鳥集》，例如江南、輔新、漢風等出版社的版本，但都不署譯者名字，且書名一律都改為《漂鳥集》，也是因為糜文開的緣故。至今兩岸新譯本不絕，但無論譯者是誰，中國至今仍以《飛鳥集》為主流，臺灣還是繼續稱為《漂鳥集》，兩岸各有定譯，也是頗為有趣的現象。

　　糜文開 (1908–1983) 是江蘇無錫人，中華民國外交官，1940 年代長駐印度，也在印度國際大學哲學系進修，與印度淵源甚深。1948 年，他在印度大使館長夏無事，和同事容寶琛兩人偶然發現鄭振鐸的《飛鳥集》不全，且誤譯處不少，於是重譯此書，改書名為《漂鳥集》，理由是「漂鳥」比「飛鳥」更符合印度崇尚雲遊漂泊修行者的意象。序中說當初翻譯此詩集純為「消夏」，初無出版之計畫，他比較急於出版的是 1948 年上半年已經譯完的 《奈都夫人詩全集》。為了這本詩集，他不但跟作者奈都夫人

合照，夫人也寫了幾句給中文讀者的話，又請了駐印度大使羅家倫寫序，一切準備妥當，寄去上海商務準備出版。誰知 1949 年時局大亂，上海商務說無法出版了，糜文開羈留香港，只好自己開起出版社來。出版社叫做「印度研究社」，專出糜文開和女兒糜榴麗兩人譯作。原本計畫出五本書，第五本即《泰戈爾詩總集》，包含已譯完的《漂鳥集》和《新月集》，不過後來只出了前四種，《泰戈爾詩總集》並未在香港出版。

糜文開 1953 年來到臺灣，繼續外交官生涯，也在大學教印度文學。1955 年，應朋友要求，在香港大學《生活月刊》連載早已譯出的《漂鳥集》，許多讀者為之驚豔，三民書局遂在 1956 年出版《漂鳥集》單行本。此後「漂鳥」成為臺灣的定譯，儘管臺灣還有周策縱在美國譯的《失群的鳥》和羅青的《單飛的鳥》，但都無法取代《漂鳥集》在讀者心

中的地位。糜文開與糜榴麗父女合譯的《新月集》
也繼《漂鳥集》後出版。糜文開又陸續與夫人裴溥
言合譯其他五冊泰戈爾詩集，1958 年出齊七冊。此
時距離他在新德里消夏時翻譯《漂鳥集》已有十年，
他自己漂泊港臺，歷經喪偶與新婚，境遇憂喜交織，
恍若隔世，也見證了戰後文人流離遷徙的動亂時光。

　　《漂鳥集》和《新月集》風格完全不同。《漂鳥
集》是精緻玲瓏的浮光掠影，短短一兩句人生哲理
沁人心脾，的確足以「消夏」；《新月集》卻是童趣
十足，親子情深之作，幾首敘事詩有情有景，難以
忘懷。每一本譯作都與譯者的生命歷程交織而成，
今天重看糜文開翻譯的泰戈爾詩作，似乎還能感受
到 1948 年印度的那一個漫漫長夏呢！

師大翻譯研究所教授　賴慈芸

二〇一八年三月

序

　　要了解一位大詩人的詩，須先了解他的生平及思想，詩哲泰戈爾的詩，雖然清新俊逸，但是你若不了解他奧妙哲學的全部，便不能有真切的了解，而且有好些詩你會完全不知所云。 泰戈爾自獲得1913 年的諾貝爾文學獎金以後，他的詩風靡全球，不到十年 ， 也引起了中國新文壇的狂熱 ， 尤其在1924 年他來華的前後，有許多文藝工作者搶著譯他的書，許多書店搶著出版他的譯本。他的好多重要著作有了中譯本，而且同一著作有的有著幾個中譯本，真是盛極一時。但是因為是趕時髦搶譯，有的譯本，未免草率，以致錯誤百出。就是認真從事的，也因了解不足，還是譯得不妥貼，甚至到處出岔子。

拿鄭振鐸所譯《飛鳥集》為例，他譯這集子時，已有人選譯過，他擬全譯，但化了許多時間全譯後因無把握，仍刪節為選譯本，刪去難譯的詩達六十八首之多。譯成後又由葉聖陶、徐玉諾二位仔細校讀過，而且他又給泰翁寫傳記，可謂對泰翁有專門研究的人了，但是他仍免不了草率，免不了誤解。Stray Birds 譯為飛鳥便不能妥貼，有好幾首誤解了原意，第六十八首 Wrong cannot afford defeat, but Right can. 譯為「錯誤不會招失敗，但是真理卻會。」竟是原意的反面，真要使人吃驚。至於草率到 dusk 錯認為 dust，於二八一及三一四等首均把這字一再譯為「煙塵」，三二五首中的 cling 誤認為 climb 而譯為「爬」，三二四首中的 tract 誤認為 track 而譯為「轍跡」，二一八首的 shadowy 認為 shady 而譯為「蔭涼的」，不勝枚舉，真是太不負責任了。至於三十八首中的 limbs 譯為「唇」，一四四

首中的 sings 譯為「嘆」，或者是未照原文譯，或者是被手民所誤。

我在國內時，曾陸續看過好多泰翁作品的中譯本，及有關泰翁的理論及傳記，到印後六年間，又把他重要著作的英文本逐一閱讀，我雖有把奈都夫人的詩和迦里陀莎的劇本譯成中文的奢望，但從未想起要把泰翁的作品重譯，因為翻譯泰翁作品的有很多人是名家，是我向所信賴的。

新德里夏季的炎熱，頗不宜於文字的寫作，照例有錢的人都上山避暑去了，不去避暑的人也只上午做些事，下午便家家閉戶，行人絕跡，鬧市一變而為死市，若有人敢驅車出門巡禮一番，一定說這裡是一座鬼城，因為一切動物也都成蟄伏狀態，連一條狗一隻貓也看不到，飛鳥走獸，都已蟄伏在隱蔽的地方了。我雖從未避暑，但到新德里後，夏季也總看點閒書消遣。今夏寶琛兄看中了我桌上的

Stray Birds，讀得很有興趣，我便把鄭譯《飛鳥集》
找給他，勸他試把鄭譯所缺六十八首譯出來，因為
這六十八首大半是這書精彩的部分。寶琛兄要我幫
著一同譯。我們把鄭譯與英文本對著，發現鄭書已
譯的部分，錯誤很多，於是我決定在辦公之後以消
閒的態度，參考鄭譯，把全書三二六首逐一譯出，
我每天譯上二三首，或四五首，寶琛兄便幫我繕正，
覺得這樣消夏，精神很愉快。英國詩人夏芝曾遇到
一位印度醫生對他說：「我每天讀了泰戈爾的一句
詩，世上的一切苦痛便立刻忘了。」我也真的把炎
熱都忘了。

　　我對泰戈爾的哲學有相當的理解，懂得他對宇
宙萬物的看法，懂得他「死是生命的一部分」的道
理，懂得他「醜是不完全的美」、「惡是不完全的善」
的意思，懂得「真相」、「假相」的分別，以及他對
「上帝」的認識等等，所以譯起來並不覺得十分困

難，興趣濃厚時，在盛暑中一天譯上十多首而不倦，因此不到兩個月，我便把全書譯完了。

泰翁這本詩集，可說是雋品中的雋品，很受中國讀者的歡迎，對中國文壇的影響很大，曾引起冰心女士等專寫小詩的風氣。但其中有好幾首，簡直不是詩，只是格言，前舉第六十八首便是一例，我們雖然都譯出了，但決不可當做詩讀。有幾首詩原文可以有兩種解釋而都合於泰翁的觀點的，我便採取與鄭譯不同的一種。

可是書名應該怎樣譯法呢？鄭譯「飛鳥」固不妥貼，一般譯作「迷鳥」更不適切，如譯「偶來的鳥」又嫌用字太拙，我擬譯為「漂鳥」，但不知是否貼切，我便設法找孟加拉文原作來研究，但他孟加拉文著作的書目中，沒有相當這本詩的書名，特地向幾位印度學者請教，他們也回答不出來，我看到他第二首詩便是嚮往於漂泊者的話，更想到古代印

度學者修道的四階段，最後是雲遊期，尚在林棲期之後，而印度兩大史詩至今尚有流浪詩人挨戶來歌唱。可知印人對雲遊的重視，對漂泊者的尊敬了。這書第一首以漂鳥象徵經過森林裡修道後的雲遊者確甚適切，再經查動物學書，知唱歌的鶯類，便是漂鳥之一種，與詩句完全符合，於是決定譯作「漂鳥」。我把我這個意見告訴印度朋友，也獲得好些人的讚許。

鄭振鐸等在二十多年前已給我們做了不少開路的工作，縱有誤譯，也應原諒，像大詩人泰戈爾的作品，有很多中譯本已絕版了，而且到今朝也應該是重新把它們有系統地精譯出版的時期了。但在今日的出版條件中，頗覺困難，我譯這本書，也只是為了消夏，並不是為了應市。現在只記下我翻譯的經過，留作紀念，將來有興致時，不妨再拿出來讀讀，修改幾首，潤飾幾字，以求格外完美，以後如

有閒暇，或者也將再譯幾本，自然有出版的機會，也不妨就印它出來，至於對絕版書的補救，我想可以精選泰戈爾的代表作，包括詩歌、戲劇與小說，出一本集子，以饗讀者。可能時我當盡力試他一下。

文開

民國三十七年八月十日於新德里

1

夏天的漂鳥，到我窗前來唱歌，又飛去了。

秋天的黃葉，沒有歌唱，只嘆息一聲，飄落在那裡。

Stray birds of summer come to my window to sing and fly away.

And yellow leaves of autumn, which have no songs, flutter and fall there with a sigh.

2

世界上渺小的漂泊者之群啊，留下你們的足印在我的字句裡吧。

O troupe of little vagrants of the world, leave your footprints in my words.

3

世界在愛人面前把他龐大的面具卸下。

他變成渺小得像一支歌,像一個永恆的接吻。

The world puts off its mask of vastness to its lover.

It becomes small as one song, as one kiss of the eternal.

4

這是大地的淚水保持著她的微笑盛放。

It is the tears of the earth that keep her smiles in bloom.

5

廣大的沙漠為著搖搖頭笑笑就飛逃的一葉青草而燃燒著愛情之火。

The mighty desert is burning for the love of a blade of grass who shakes her head and laughs and flies away.

6

假使當你渴念著太陽而流淚,那末你也在渴念著星星啊。

If you shed tears when you miss the sun, you also miss the stars.

7

跳舞著的水啊,在你途中的砂粒乞求你的唱歌和流動。
你願擔起他們跛者的負荷嗎?

The sands in your way beg for your song and your movement, dancing water. Will you carry the burden of their lameness?

8

她的渴望的臉像夜雨般纏繞住我的清夢。

Her wistful face haunts my dreams like the rain at night.

9

從前我們曾夢見我們都是陌路人。

當我們醒來時卻發見我們互相親愛著。

Once we dreamt that we were strangers.

We wake up to find that we were dear to each other.

10

正像「黃昏」在靜寂的林中，「憂愁」在我的心裡已平靜下去。

Sorrow is hushed into peace in my heart like the evening among the silent trees.

11

有些看不見的手指，像閒逸的微風，在我心上奏著漪波
的音樂。

Some unseen fingers, like an idle breeze, are playing
upon my heart the music of the ripples.

12

「海喲，你講的什麼話？」

「是永遠疑問的話。」

「天喲，什麼是你回答的話？」

「是永遠的沉默。」

"What language is thine, O sea?"

"The language of eternal question."

"What language is thy answer, O sky?"

"The language of eternal silence."

13

我的心，請靜聽世界的低語，那是他在對你談愛啊。

Listen, my heart, to the whispers of the world with
which it makes love to you.

14

造化的奧祕有如夜的黝黑——這是偉大的。智識的迷惘只是清晨的霧。

The mystery of creation is like the darkness of night—it is great. Delusions of knowledge are like the fog of the morning.

15

不要把你的愛置於絕壁之上,因為那是很高的。

Do not seat your love upon a precipice because it is high.

16

今晨我坐在我的窗口,世界像一個過路人在那裡停留片刻,向我點點頭又走開了。

I sit at my window this morning where the world like a passer-by stops for a moment, nods to me and goes.

17

這些小小的思想是那沙沙的樹葉聲；它們有它們愉悅的
低語在我的心裡。

These little thoughts are the rustle of leaves; they have
their whisper of joy in my mind.

18

你是什麼，你看不見，你所看見的只是你的影子。

What you are you do not see, what you see is your
shadow.

19

我的願望都是愚蠢的，他們呼喊得掩蓋了你的歌聲，我主。

讓我只靜聽著吧。

My wishes are fools, they shout across thy songs, my Master.

Let me but listen.

20

我不能挑選最好的。

是最好的挑選我。

I cannot choose the best.

The best chooses me.

21

那些把燈籠揹在後面的人，將他們的影子投在他們的前面。

They throw their shadows before them who carry their lantern on their back.

22

我的存在是一個永恆的奇異，那就是生命。

That I exist is a perpetual surprise which is life.

23

「我們樹葉子有沙沙的聲音去回答風雨，可是你是誰啊，
這樣的沉默？」

「我只是一朵花。」

"We, the rustling leaves, have a voice that answers the
storms, but who are you so silent?"

"I am a mere flower."

24

休息之屬於勞動，正如眼瞼之屬於眼睛。

Rest belongs to the work as the eyelids to the eyes.

25

人是一個才出生的嬰孩，他的力量就是生長的力量。

Man is a born child, his power is the power of growth.

26

上帝期待著得到回答是為了他送給我們的鮮花，並不是
為了太陽或土地。

God expects answers for the flowers he sends us, not for
the sun and the earth.

27

遊戲著的光正像一個赤裸的小孩，歡樂地在綠葉叢中，
他是不曉得大人會說謊的。

The light that plays, like a naked child, among the
green leaves happily knows not that man can lie.

28

啊，美啊，你要從愛之中去發見你自己，不要向你那鏡子的阿諛中去追求。

O beauty, find thyself in love, not in the flattery of thy mirror.

29

我的心衝激著她的波浪在世界的岸邊上，在那上面用淚水寫上她的簽名：「我愛你。」

My heart beats her waves at the shore of the world and writes upon it her signature in tears with the words, "I love thee."

30

「月亮你在等著什麼呢？」

「要向我必須為他讓路的太陽致敬。」

"Moon, for what do you wait?"

"To salute the sun for whom I must make way."

31

樹木像是沉默的大地的渴望之音來到我的窗前。

The trees come up to my window like the yearning voice of the dumb earth.

32

對於上帝，他自己所造的每一個清晨都是一種新的奇蹟。

His own mornings are new surprises to God.

33

生命因世界的需要而發見它的財富，因愛的需要而發見它的價值。

Life finds its wealth by the claims of the world, and its worth by the claims of love.

34

乾涸的河床覺得毋須感謝它的過去。

The dry river-bed finds no thanks for its past.

35

鳥兒希望它是一朵雲。

雲兒希望它是一隻鳥。

The bird wishes it were a cloud.

The cloud wishes it were a bird.

36

瀑布唱道:「我得到自由時我便唱出歌來了。」

The waterfall sings, "I find my song, when I find my freedom."

37

我不能夠說出為什麼這顆心默然憔悴。

是為了那些他永不請求，永不認識，永不記著的小小需要而憔悴。

I cannot tell why this heart languishes in silence.

It is for small needs it never asks, or knows or remembers.

38

女人，當你走動著料理家事時你的手腳都在唱歌，像一條山溪在卵石中歌唱一般。

Woman, when you move about in your household service your limbs sing like a hill stream among its pebbles.

39

太陽橫跨西海走去，留著他向東方的最後問候。

The sun goes to cross the Western sea, leaving its last salutation to the East.

40

不要因你無食慾而譴責你的食物。

Do not blame your food because you have no appetite.

41

樹木像是渴慕的大地翹盼著天堂。

The trees, like the longings of the earth, stand a-tiptoe to peep at the heaven.

42

你微笑著而不對我說什麼，我覺得這就是我已經久候的。

You smiled and talked to me of nothing and I felt that for this I had been waiting long.

43

水裡的魚是靜寂的，陸上的獸是喧擾的，空中的鳥是唱著的。

但是人卻具有了海水的靜寂，陸地的喧擾，和天空的音樂。

The fish in the water is silent, the animal on the earth is noisy, the bird in the air is singing.

But Man has in him the silence of the sea, the noise of the earth and the music of the air.

44

世界衝越過纏綿的心絃彈奏著憂鬱的音樂。

The world rushes on over the strings of the lingering heart making the music of sadness.

45

他把他的武器當做他的上帝。

他本身是失敗了，當他武器勝利的時候。

He has made his weapons his gods.

When his weapons win he is defeated himself.

46

從創造中上帝發見他自己。

God finds himself by creating.

47

陰影戴著面幕，祕密地，溫順地，躡著她靜寂的愛之步，
隨從在光的後面。

Shadow, with her veil drawn, follows Light in secret
meekness, with her silent steps of love.

48

星星不因僅似螢火而怯於出現。

The stars are not afraid to appear like fireflies.

49

我感謝你，我不是一個權力的車輪，但我卻是被這車輪
所輾壓的活的生物之一。

I thank thee that I am none of the wheels of power but
I am one with the living creatures that are crushed by it.

50

這顆銳而不寬的心，觸到每一個地方，但並未移動。

The mind, sharp but not broad, sticks at every point but
does not move.

51

你的偶像被粉碎在塵埃中，這證明上帝的塵埃比你的偶
像偉大。

Your idol is shattered in the dust to prove that God's
dust is greater than your idol.

52

人沒有把他自己顯示到他的歷史中，他只在掙扎著通過
他的歷史。

Man does not reveal himself in his history, he struggles
up through it.

53

玻璃燈斥責瓦燈稱他做表兄，但當月亮上升，那玻璃燈
卻溫和地微笑著招呼她：「我親愛的，親愛的姐姐。」

While the glass lamp rebukes the earthen for calling it
cousin, the moon rises, and the glass lamp, with a bland
smile, calls her,—"My dear, dear sister."

54

似海鷗與波浪的會合，我們相會，我們親近。似海鷗的
飛去，波浪的盪開，我們分離。

Like the meeting of the seagulls and the waves we meet
and come near. The seagulls fly off, the waves roll away
and we depart.

55

做完了我白天的工作，我便像一隻拖放在岸灘上的小船
似地，靜聽著晚潮跳舞的音樂。

My day is done, and I am like a boat drawn on the
beach, listening to the dance-music of the tide in the
evening.

56

生命授與我們，但我們須付出生命才能得到生命。

Life is given to us, we earn it by giving it.

57

當我們十二分謙遜之時，便是我們最接近偉大之時。

We come nearest to the great when we are great in humility.

58

麻雀因孔雀拖著重累的尾巴而替牠可憐。

The sparrow is sorry for the peacock at the burden of its tail.

59

永勿懼怕那瞬息——這就是永久唱出的歌聲。

Never be afraid of the moments—thus sings the voice of the everlasting.

60

颶風於無路處尋覓著最短的途徑，又突然在「烏有鄉」
停止了他的尋覓。

The hurricane seeks the shortest road by the no-road,
and suddenly ends its search in the Nowhere.

61

朋友，請就在我的杯中飲了我的酒吧。
當它傾入別的杯裡，它的泡沫圈兒便消失了。

Take my wine in my own cup, friend.
It loses its wreath of foam when poured into that of
others.

62

「完善」因「缺陷」的愛，把她自己裝飾得美麗。

The Perfect decks itself in beauty for the love of the
Imperfect.

63

上帝對人說:「我醫治你所以我要損傷你,我愛你所以我要處罰你。」

God says to man, "I heal you therefore I hurt, love you therefore punish."

64

感謝火焰的光,但不要忘記那沉著而堅毅地站在黑影中的燈臺啊!

Thank the flame for its light, but do not forget the lampholder standing in the shade with constancy of patience.

65

小小的青草,你的步子是小的,但你占有了你踏過的土地。

Tiny grass, your steps are small, but you possess the earth under your tread.

66

嬌嫩的花張開了她的花蕾喊著:「親愛的世界啊,請勿凋謝。」

The infant flower opens its bud and cries, "Dear World, please do not fade."

67

上帝對強大的王國生厭,卻永不厭惡於小小的花朵。

God grows weary of great kingdoms, but never of little flowers.

68

邪惡經不起敗創,正義卻可以。

Wrong cannot afford defeat but Right can.

69

「我很高興奉獻了所有的水，」瀑布歌唱：「雖然少許水已足供人止渴。」

"I give my whole water in joy," sings the waterfall, "though little of it is enough for the thirsty."

70

何處是那狂歡地不停噴發著拋送起這些花朵的源泉呀？

Where is the fountain that throws up these flowers in a ceaseless outbreak of ecstasy?

71

樵夫的斧頭向樹求取他的斧柄。

樹給了他。

The woodcutter's axe begged for its handle from the tree.

The tree gave it.

72

在我寂寥的心中我感覺到幕著霧與雨的嫠婦之黃昏的嘆息。

In my solitude of heart I feel the sigh of this widowed evening veiled with mist and rain.

73

貞操是一種財富，那是充沛的愛情之產物。

Chastity is a wealth that comes from abundance of love.

74

霧像愛情一般，在山的心上遊戲，呈現著美的種種奇妙。

The mist, like love, plays upon the heart of the hills and brings out surprises of beauty.

75

我們對世界判斷錯了，所以說他是欺騙了我們。

We read the world wrong and say that it deceives us.

76

詩人的風是吹出去越海穿林來尋求他自己的歌聲的。

The poet wind is out over the sea and the forest to seek his own voice.

77

每個嬰孩的出世都帶來了上帝對人類並未失望的消息。

Every child comes with the message that God is not yet discouraged of man.

78

青草尋求著她陸地上的擁擠。

樹木尋求著他天空中的幽靜。

The grass seeks her crowd in the earth.

The tree seeks his solitude of the sky.

79

人常阻塞著他自己的路。

Man barricades against himself.

80

我的朋友,你的聲音在我心裡低迴不失,像海的喃喃聲繚繞在靜聽著的松林間。

Your voice, my friend, wanders in my heart, like the muffled sound of the sea among these listening pines.

81

黑暗中的火花是天上的繁星,但是那爆發火花的看不見的火焰是什麼呢?

What is this unseen flame of darkness whose sparks are the stars?

82

讓生時麗似夏花，死時美如秋葉。

Let life be beautiful like summer flowers and death like autumn leaves.

83

那想要做善事的人去敲著大門，那仁愛的人看見大門正開著。

He who wants to do good knocks at the gate; he who loves finds the gate open.

84

在死之中，多數合一，在生之中，一化成多數。

當上帝死去，宗教將合而為一。

In death the many becomes one; in life the one becomes many.

Religion will be one when God is dead.

85

藝術家是「自然」的愛人，所以他是自然的奴隸，又是
自然的主人。

The artist is the lover of Nature, therefore he is her
slave and her master.

86

「果實啊，你離我多遠？」

「花啊，我就藏在你的心裡呢。」

"How far are you from me, O Fruit?"

"I am hidden in your heart, O Flower."

87

渴望著的是在黑暗中覺得而在白天看不見的那個。

This longing is for the one who is felt in the dark, but
not seen in the day.

88

露水對湖沼說:「你是蓮葉下面的大水滴,我是蓮葉上面
的小水滴。」

"You are the big drop of dew under the lotus leaf, I am
the smaller one on its upper side," said the dewdrop to
the lake.

89

鋒利的劍需要鞘的庇蔭,鞘就滿足於他的魯鈍了。

The scabbard is content to be dull when it protects the
keenness of the sword.

90

在黑暗中「一」顯得混同,在光明裡「一」才顯出多樣來。

In darkness the One appears as uniform; in the light the
One appears as manifold.

91

大地得青草的幫助而變成可居住之所。

The great earth makes herself hospitable with the help
of the grass.

92

葉的誕生與死都是旋風的急速之轉動，它的廣大的圓圈
在星座間慢慢地移著。

The birth and death of the leaves are the rapid whirls of
the eddy whose wider circles move slowly among stars.

93

權力對世界說：「你屬於我。」

世界把他俘繫在她的寶座上。

仁愛對世界說：「我屬於你。」

世界給他出入她寓所的自由。

Power said to the world, "You are mine."

The world kept it prisoner on her throne.

Love said to the world, "I am thine."

The world gave it the freedom of her house.

94

霧像是大地的慾望。

他遮蔽了大地哭喊著要的太陽。

The mist is like the earth's desire.

It hides the sun for whom she cries.

95

別作聲，我的心，這許多大樹正在做禱告呢。

Be still, my heart, these great trees are prayers.

96

頃刻的喧鬧譏笑著永久的音樂。

The noise of the moment scoffs at the music of the Eternal.

97

我想到那漂浮在生與愛及死的溪流上的別的年代都被忘了，我覺到逝去的自由。

I think of other ages that floated upon the stream of life and love and death and are forgotten, and I feel the freedom of passing away.

98

我靈魂的憂鬱是她的結婚面紗。

這面紗等著天晚才揭去。

The sadness of my soul is her bride's veil.

It waits to be lifted in the night.

99

死的印記給予生的貨幣以價值；可以把生命去購買那真正的貨物。

Death's stamp gives value to the coin of life; making it possible to buy with life what is truly precious.

100

雲謙卑地站在天之一隅。

黎明用光彩作王冠來給他戴上。

The cloud stood humbly in a corner of the sky.

The morning crowned it with splendour.

101

塵土被侮辱,卻報以鮮花。

The dust receives insult and in return offers her flowers.

102

只管向前走吧,不必逗留著去採集鮮花攜帶著,因為鮮花會一路盛開著在你的前途的。

Do not linger to gather flowers to keep them, but walk on, for flowers will keep themselves blooming all your way.

103

根是生入地裡的枝。

枝是生在空中的根。

Roots are the branches down in the earth.

Branches are roots in the air.

104

那遙遠的夏之音樂，環繞著「秋天」撲翅尋求牠的舊巢。

The music of the far-away summer flutters around the
Autumn seeking its former nest.

105

不要從你的衣袋裡把功績借給你的朋友，這是侮辱他的。

Do not insult your friend by lending him merits from
your own pocket.

106

不可名時日的接觸，像環繞老樹的蘚苔般依附著我的心。

The touch of the nameless days clings to my heart like
mosses round the old tree.

107

回聲譏笑她的原聲去證明她是原來的聲音。

The echo mocks her origin to prove she is the original.

108

當幸運兒誇張著上帝的特別恩典時，上帝是慚愧的。

God is ashamed when the prosperous boasts of His special favour.

109

我將我自己的影子拋在我的路上，因為我有一盞沒有點燃的明燈。

I cast my own shadow upon my path, because I have a lamp that has not been lighted.

110

個人加入熱鬧的群眾，去淹沒他自己的靜默之喧聲。

Man goes into the noisy crowd to drown his own clamour of silence.

111

疲乏的盡頭是死，但完善的盡頭是無盡。

That which ends in exhaustion is death, but the perfect ending is in the endless.

112

太陽只有單純的光之外衣。雲霞卻被華麗所裝飾。

The sun has his simple robe of light. The clouds are decked with gorgeousness.

113

山峰正如群兒的呼喊，高舉著手臂，想要攬捉星星。

The hills are like shouts of children who raise their arms, trying to catch stars.

114

行人雖擁擠，路是寂寞的，因為沒有人愛他。

The road is lonely in its crowd, for it is not loved.

115

權力自誇他的禍害，為落地的黃葉與過路的閒雲所笑。

The power that boasts of its mischiefs is laughed at by the yellow leaves that fall, and clouds that pass by.

116

今天，大地像是一個在太陽裡紡紗的婦人，她用那忘卻的語言對我低唱著一些古歌。

The earth hums to me to-day in the sun, like a woman at her spinning, some ballad of the ancient time in a forgotten tongue.

117

草葉值得生長在這偉大的世界上。

The grass-blade is worthy of the great world where it grows.

118

夢是一位妻子，她定要說話，

睡眠是一位丈夫，他默不作聲地忍受著。

Dream is a wife who must talk.

Sleep is a husband who silently suffers.

119

黑夜吻著消逝的白日，在他的耳邊低語道：「我是死亡，是你的母親。我正給你新的誕生。」

The night kisses the fading day whispering to his ear, "I am death, your mother. I am to give you fresh birth."

120

黑夜啊，我感覺到你美麗，正像那被愛的少婦吹熄了她的燈時一樣。

I feel thy beauty, dark night, like that of the loved woman when she has put out the lamp.

121

我把衰敗的世界帶進我繁榮的世界裡。

I carry in my world that flourishes the worlds that have failed.

122

親愛的朋友，當我傾聽濤聲時，我便感覺到你在這海灘上許多個深晚的偉大思想的平靜了。

Dear friend, I feel the silence of your great thoughts of many a deepening eventide on this beach when I listen to these waves.

123

飛鳥想這是善舉，如果把魚兒舉入高空。

The bird thinks it is an act of kindness to give the fish a lift in the air.

124

夜對太陽說：「你在明月裡送給我你的情書，我把我含淚的答覆留在草上了。」

"In the moon thou sendest thy love letters to me," said the night to the sun.

"I leave my answers in tears upon the grass."

125

「偉大」生來是一個小兒；當他死時，他把他偉大的童年留給世界。

The Great is a born child; when he dies he gives his great childhood to the world.

126

不是鐵鎚的敲打能奏效的，只有那水的跳舞的歌聲，能使石卵臻於完美。

Not hammer-strokes, but dance of the water sings the pebbles into perfection.

127

蜜蜂吮吸花蜜，當他離開時便嗡嗡地鳴謝著。

華麗的蝴蝶深信花朵欠禮，應該謝他。

Bees sip honey from flowers and hum their thanks when they leave.

The gaudy butterfly is sure that the flowers owe thanks to him.

128

要侃侃而談是容易的，假使你不等說出完全的真理。

To be outspoken is easy when you do not wait to speak the complete truth.

129

「可能」問「不可能」說：「何處是你的寓所？」

得到的回答是：「在無能者的夢裡。」

Asks the Possible to the Impossible, "Where is your dwelling-place?"

"In the dreams of the impotent," comes the answer.

130

如果你對一切怪論深閉固拒，真理也要被關在門外了。

If you shut your door to all errors truth will be shut out.

131

我聽見有什麼東西的颼颼聲在我憂鬱的心的後面響
著──但是我看不見什麼。

I hear some rustle of things behind my sadness of
heart,—I cannot see them.

132

在活動著的閒暇便是工作。

靜止的海水激動成波濤。

Leisure in its activity is work.

The stillness of the sea stirs in waves.

133

葉兒在戀愛時變成花。

花兒在崇拜時變成果。

The leaf becomes flower when it loves.

The flower becomes fruit when it worships.

134

地下的樹根並不因為使樹枝滿生果實而需要酬報。

The roots below the earth claim no rewards for making the branches fruitful.

135

在這風吹不息的雨夜，我看著搖曳的樹枝，想到萬有的偉大。

This rainy evening the wind is restless.

I look at the swaying branches and ponder over the greatness of all things.

136

午夜的暴風雨，像一個巨人的小孩，在不合時的黑暗中醒來，便開始玩耍而喧鬧了。

Storm of midnight, like a giant child awakened in the untimely dark, has begun to play and shout.

137

哦，海啊，你掀起你的波濤來也追不到你的情人啊，你
這孤寂的風暴之新婦。

Thou raisest thy waves vainly to follow thy lover, O sea,
thou lonely bride of the storm.

138

「文字」對「工作」說：「我羞愧著我的空虛。」

「工作」對「文字」說：「當我一見到你，我知道我是何
等的貧乏了。」

"I am ashamed of my emptiness," said the Word to the
Work.

"I know how poor I am when I see you," said the
Work to the Word.

139

時間是變更的財富，但時鐘的哼著諧詩，單只是變更，
並無財富可言。

Time is the wealth of change, but the clock in its
parody makes it mere change and no wealth.

140

真理穿她的衣服，發覺它實在太緊窄。
在想像中，她卻轉動得舒適自如。

Truth in her dress finds facts too tight.
In fiction she moves with ease.

141

哦，路啊，當我僕僕風塵於這裡和那裡，我是討厭你的，
可是現在你領導我走向各處去，我已因愛情而與你結合了。

When I travelled to here and to there, I was tired of
thee, O Road, but now when thou leadest me to
everywhere I am wedded to thee in love.

142

讓我設想，在那群星中間，有一顆星正引導我的生命通過那黑暗的未知。

Let me think that there is one among those stars that guides my life through the dark unknown.

143

婦人啊，你優雅的手指接觸到了我的器物，便井然有秩像音樂般有節奏之美了。

Woman, with the grace of your fingers you touched my things and order came out like music.

144

一種憂傷的聲音營巢於多年的廢墟間。

在夜裡，那聲音向我唱著：「我愛過你。」

One sad voice has its nest among the ruins of the years.

It sings to me in the night,—"I loved you."

145

熊熊的烈火用他延燒的火舌警告我走開。

請從埋在灰中的餘燼裡救我出來。

The flaming fire warns me off by its own glow.

Save me from the dying embers hidden under ashes.

146

我有空中的星星，

但是，哦，卻想念我室內未點的小燈。

I have my stars in the sky,

But oh for my little lamp unlit in my house.

147

死去的文字之遺灰黏附著你。

將靜默來洗滌你的靈魂吧。

The dust of the dead words clings to thee.

Wash thy soul with silence.

148

裂口留在生命裡，死亡的哀歌就從裂口送出來。

Gaps are left in life through which comes the sad music of death.

149

世界已在清晨打開了他光煥的心。

出來吧，我的心，用你的愛迎接他。

The world has opened its heart of light in the morning.

Come out, my heart, with thy love to meet it.

150

我的思想與這些閃光的葉子一起閃耀著，我的心由於陽光的接觸而唱著；我的生命因得與萬物一起飄浮進空間的蔚藍，飄浮進時間的黝黑而欣喜著。

My thoughts shimmer with these shimmering leaves and my heart sings with the touch of this sunlight; my life is glad to be floating with all things into the blue of space, into the dark of time.

151

上帝的大權力是寓於和風中，並不在暴風雨裡。

God's great power is in the gentle breeze, not in the storm.

152

這是一場夢，一切事物都散漫著都緊壓著我。當我醒來，我將見到它們都已聚集在你那裡，那末，我便得自由了。

This is a dream in which things are all loose and they oppress. I shall find them gathered in thee when I awake and shall be free.

153

「誰來接替我的職務？」落日詢問。

「我將盡力做去，我主。」瓦燈說。

"Who is there to take up my duties?" asked the setting sun.

"I shall do what I can, my Master," said the earthen lamp.

154

你摘取花瓣並未採集著花的美麗。

By plucking her petals you do not gather the beauty of the flower.

155

靜默將負載你的聲音，有如鳥巢支持著睡鳥。

Silence will carry your voice like the nest that holds the sleeping birds.

156

「偉大」不怕與「渺小」同行。

只有中間才遠離別人。

The Great walks with the Small without fear.

The Middling keeps aloof.

157

黑夜暗中把花朵開放而讓白日接受謝意。

The night opens the flowers in secret and allows the day to get thanks.

158

權力把它犧牲者的掙扎當做是忘恩。

Power takes as ingratitude the writhings of its victims.

159

當我們滿足地樂意時，我們就可以愉快地帶著我們的果實分開了。

When we rejoice in our fulness, then we can part with our fruits with joy.

160

雨點吻著大地,低語道:「母親啊,我們是你的有思家病
的孩子,從天上回到你的懷抱了。」

The raindrops kissed the earth and whispered, — "We
are thy homesick children, mother, come back to thee
from the heaven."

161

蛛網要捕捉蒼蠅,卻假裝著捕捉露珠。

The cobweb pretends to catch dew-drops and catches
flies.

162

「愛」啊！當我來時因你手中正燃燒著的愁苦之燈我得看見你的面色，並且知道你就是「快樂」。

Love! When you come with the burning lamp of pain in your hand, I can see your face and know you as bliss.

163

螢火對星星說：「學者說你的光將有熄滅的一天。」

星星沒有回答。

"The learned say that your lights will one day be no more," said the firefly to the stars.

The stars made no answer.

164

一隻黎明之鳥在這黃昏的薄暗中飛到我靜寂之巢來。

In the dusk of the evening the bird of some early dawn comes to the nest of my silence.

165

思想透澈我的心頭正如雁群掠過天空。

我聽見牠們的翼聲。

Thoughts pass in my mind like flocks of ducks in the sky.

I hear the voice of their wings.

166

運河歡喜想著那河流是專為供給他河水而存在的。

The canal loves to think that rivers exist solely to supply it with water.

167

世界以痛苦吻我靈魂，卻要求報以詩歌。

The world has kissed my soul with its pain, asking for its return in songs.

168

那在壓迫著我的到底是我的靈魂想要出來到空曠之處去
呢，還是那世界的靈魂敲著我的心門想要進去呢？

That which oppresses me, is it my soul trying to come
out in the open, or the soul of the world knocking at
my heart for its entrance?

169

思想用它自己的文字培養它自己而滋長著。

Thought feeds itself with its own words and grows.

170

我把我的心之缸浸入這靜默之時間中，它已充滿著愛了。

I have dipped the vessel of my heart into this silent
hour; it has filled with love.

171

不管你有沒有工作。

當你一說「讓我們做點事吧」，那時就開始在惡作劇了。

Either you have work or you have not.

When you have to say, "Let us do something," then begins mischief.

172

向日葵因承認那無名之花是她的親戚而羞愧。

太陽上升時卻對無名之花含笑地說：「我的愛人，你好不好？」

The sunflower blushed to own the nameless flower as her kin.

The sun rose and smiled on it, saying, "Are you well, my darling?"

173

「是誰像命運一樣驅遣著我？」

「是『自我』跨在我的背上。」

"Who drives me forward like fate?"

"The Myself striding on my back."

174

雲兒把河之水杯注滿；自己卻隱藏在遠處的山中。

The clouds fill the watercups of the river, hiding themselves in the distant hills.

175

在取水的途中，我把我水瓶裡的水潑掉了。

很少水剩留下來以供家用。

I spill water from my water jar as I walk on my way.

Very little remains for my home.

176

在缸裡的水是透明的；在海中的水卻黝黑。

微小的真理有清晰的言辭；偉大的真理卻只是偉大的沉默。

The water in a vessel is sparkling; the water in the sea is dark.

The small truth has words that are clear; the great truth has great silence.

177

你的微笑是你田野的花，你的談吐是你山松的蕭蕭聲，可是你的心卻是我們人人皆知的婦人。

Your smile was the flowers of your own fields, your talk was the rustle of your own mountain pines, but your heart was the woman that we all know.

178

是小東西，我把它留下給我親愛的人——大的東西則留給大眾。

It is the little things that I leave behind for my loved ones,—great things are for everyone.

179

婦人啊，你把你的奧妙的淚水包圍住世界的心有如海之
於陸地。

Woman, thou hast encircled the world's heart with the
depth of thy tears as the sea has the earth.

180

陽光以微笑歡迎我。

雨，他的顰感的妹妹，對我的心談著衷曲。

The sunshine greets me with a smile.

The rain, his sad sister, talks to my heart.

181

我的白晝的花隨便地掉下它被忘的花瓣。

在晚上它長成為紀念的黃金果實。

My flower of the day dropped its petals forgotten.

In the evening it ripens into a golden fruit of memory.

182

我好像夜裡的路,在靜默中正傾聽著記憶的足音。

I am like the road in the night listening to the footfalls
of its memories in silence.

183

在我看來黃昏的天空像一個窗子,窗內點著一盞燈,裡
邊正有一個人在等待著呢!

The evening sky to me is like a window, and a lighted
lamp, and a waiting behind it.

184

太忙於做好的人往往無時間去做好。

He who is too busy doing good finds no time to be good.

185

我是無雨的秋雲,但在黃熟的稻田裡,可以見到我的充實。

I am the autumn cloud, empty of rain, see my fulness in the field of ripened rice.

186

仇恨的殘殺的,大家讚美他們。

但上帝慚愧地趕快把這記憶隱藏到綠草底下去。

They hated and killed and men praised them.

But God in shame hastens to hide its memory under the green grass.

187

足趾是不回顧過去的手指。

Toes are the fingers that have forsaken their past.

188

黑暗趨向光明,但盲目趨向死亡。

Darkness travels towards light, but blindness towards death.

189

被寵的小犬猜疑宇宙要設計取得牠的地位。

The pet dog suspects the universe for scheming to take
its place.

190

我的心啊,請安靜地坐著,不要把塵埃揚起來。

讓世界找出他到你那裡的路來。

Sit still my heart, do not raise your dust.

Let the world find its way to you.

191

弓在箭離弦前對他低語道:「你的自由是我的。」

The bow whispers to the arrow before it speeds forth—
"Your freedom is mine."

192

婦人啊，在你的笑聲裡含有生命之泉的音樂。

Woman, in your laughter you have the music of the fountain of life.

193

一個充滿邏輯的心恰像一把四面都是鋒刃的刀。

它會使那用它的手流出血來。

A mind all logic is like a knife all blade.

It makes the hand bleed that uses it.

194

上帝喜歡人的燈光甚於他自己的巨星。

God loves man's lamp-lights better than his own great stars.

195

這世界是一個粗野的暴風雨的世界，那優美的音樂使牠馴服著。

This world is the world of wild storms kept tame with the music of beauty.

196

「我的心好像你吻著的黃金寶箱。」暮雲對太陽說。

"My heart is like the golden casket of thy kiss," said the sunset cloud to the sun.

197

過分接近可能殺死；保持距離或許成功。

By touching you may kill, by keeping away you may possess.

198

蟋蟀的唧唧聲和雨點的滴瀝聲透過黑暗來到我耳中，一如夢之沙沙聲來自我已逝的青春。

The cricket's chirp and the patter of rain come to me through the dark, like the rustle of dreams from my past youth.

199

花對失去了所有星斗的晨空喊道：「我失去了我的露珠。」

"I have lost my dewdrop," cries the flower to the morning sky that has lost all its stars.

200

燃燒的木頭一面噴射著火焰，一面喊道：「這是我的花，這是我的死。」

The burning log bursts in flame and cries,—"This is my flower, my death."

201

胡蜂想鄰人蜜蜂的蜂窩太小了。

鄰人卻請他造一個更小的窩。

The wasp thinks that the honey-hive of the neighbouring bees is too small.

His neighbours ask him to build one still smaller.

202

堤岸對河流說：「我不能保留你的波浪，

讓我保留你的足印在我心裡吧。」

"I cannot keep your waves," says the bank to the river.

"Let me keep your footprints in my heart."

203

白晝與這小小地球的喧囂掩蓋住全宇宙的靜默。

The day, with the noise of this little earth, drowns the

silence of all worlds.

204

歌的感覺之無限在空中，畫的感覺之無限在地上，而詩的感覺之無限兼有空中與地上；

因為詩的文字之意義能行走，文字的音樂能飛翔。

The song feels the infinite in the air, the picture in the earth, the poem in the air and the earth;

For its words have meaning that walks and music that soars.

205

太陽向「西方」落下時，他早晨的「東方」正靜悄悄地站在他的前面。

When the sun goes down to the West, the East of his morning stands before him in silence.

206

讓我不要把我自己歪斜地對著我的世界,而使他反對我。

Let me not put myself wrongly to my world and set it against me.

207

「讚美」來羞著我,因我暗地裡求取他。

Praise shames me, for I secretly beg for it.

208

在沒有事可做時讓我不做什麼只在寧靜的深處,像那風平浪靜時的海岸之黃昏。

Let my doing nothing when I have nothing to do become untroubled in its depth of peace like the evening in the seashore when the water is silent.

209

少女啊,你的淳樸,像湖水的澄碧,顯示出你真實的深厚。

Maiden, your simplicity, like the blueness of the lake, reveals your depth of truth.

210

至善不會獨至。

它與一切俱來。

The best does not come alone.

It comes with the company of the all.

211

上帝的右手是慈和的；但他的左手是可怕的。

God's right hand is gentle, but terrible is his left hand.

212

我的黃昏來到異域的林間，說著一種我的晨星所不懂的話。

My evening came among the alien trees and spoke in a
language which my morning stars did not know.

213

夜的黑暗是一隻袋，黎明的金光從袋中爆裂開來。

Night's darkness is a bag that bursts with the gold of
the dawn.

214

我們的願望以虹霓的彩色借給僅只煙霧般的生命。

Our desire lends the colours of the rainbow to the mere mists and vapours of life.

215

上帝等待著取還他自己的花，那花由人類的手捧著作為禮物獻上去。

God waits to win back his own flowers as gifts from man's hands.

216

我的憂思困擾我，要問我他們自己的名字。

My sad thoughts tease me asking me their own names.

217

果實的職務很尊貴，花朵的職務很甜美；可是讓我的職務成為葉子的職務，謙遜地奉獻它的濃蔭吧。

The service of the fruit is precious, the service of the flower is sweet, but let my service be the service of the leaves in its shade of humble devotion.

218

我的心已張帆在閒風中，將駛向「任何地方」的幻影之島。

My heart has spread its sails to the idle winds for the shadowy island of Anywhere.

219

眾人是殘酷的；但個人是和善的。

Men are cruel, but Man is kind.

220

把我做成你的酒杯，讓我的滿杯供獻給你，供獻給你的人。

Make me thy cup and let my fulness be for thee and for thine.

221

暴風雨就像什麼神只為大地拒絕他愛的苦痛而叫喊著。

The storm is like the cry of some god in pain whose love the earth refuses.

222

世界沒有損漏，因為死並不是破裂。

The world does not leak because death is not a crack.

223

生命因失去的愛而更豐富。

Life has become richer by the love that has been lost.

224

朋友啊，你的偉大的心借「東方」的朝陽照耀著，有如黎明時孤山的雪峰。

My friend, your great heart shone with the sunrise of the East like the snowy summit of a lonely hill in the dawn.

225

死的泉源使生的止水噴放。

The fountain of death makes the still water of life play.

226

我的上帝啊，那些什麼東西都有而沒有你的人，嘲笑那
些只有你而沒有東西的人呢。

Those who have everything but thee, my God, laugh at
those who have nothing but thyself.

227

生命的活動休息在他自己的音樂中。

The movement of life has its rest in its own music.

228

踩踢著只會揚起塵埃來，不會從泥土上有出收穫來的。

Kicks only raise dust and not crops from the earth.

229

我們的名字都是黑夜的海波上生出來的閃光，死時不留
一點痕跡。

Our names are the light that glows on the sea waves at
night and then dies without leaving its signature.

230

讓睜眼看著玫瑰花的人只看見針刺。

Let him only see the thorns who has eyes to see the rose.

231

把鳥翼裝金,鳥便再不能翱翔在天空。

Set bird's wings with gold and it will never again soar in the sky.

232

和我們地方同樣的蓮花開在這異域的水中,有同樣的香氣,但換著別的名字了。

The same lotus of our clime blooms here in the alien water with the same sweetness, under another name.

233

在心的透視中距離隱約的顯得闊大。

In heart's perspective the distance looms large.

234

月亮把她的清光照耀整個天空，黑斑卻留給她自己。

The moon has her light all over the sky, her dark spots to herself.

235

不要說，「這還是早晨」，並借昨天的名義將它遣去。第二次看它，像看一個沒有名字的新生嬰孩。

Do not say, "It is morning," and dismiss it with a name of yesterday. See it for the first time as a new-born child that has no name.

236

輕煙對天空，灰燼對大地，都誇說他們是火的兄弟。

Smoke boasts to the sky, and Ashes to the earth, that they are brothers to the fire.

237

雨點向素馨花耳語：「永遠把我留在你的心裡吧。」

素馨花嘆了一聲，「噯唷！」就掉向地面去。

The raindrop whispered to the jasmine, "Keep me in your heart for ever."

The jasmine sighed, "Alas," and dropped to the ground.

238

羞怯的思想啊，請不要怕我。

我是一個詩人。

Timid thoughts, do not be afraid of me.

I am a poet.

239

我心裡模糊的靜默，似乎充滿著蟋蟀的唧唧聲——那灰色的微曦之音。

The dim silence of my mind seems filled with crickets' chirp—the grey twilight of sound.

240

流星炮啊，你對星辰的侮慢將隨著你自己回到大地。

Rockets, your insult to the stars follows yourself back to the earth.

241

你引導我從我的白天熱鬧的旅程去到黃昏的孤寂。

我從沉寂之夜等候這事的意義。

Thou hast led me through my crowded travels of the day to my evening's loneliness.

I wait for its meaning through the stillness of the night.

242

生命如渡過一重大海，我們相遇在這同一的狹船裡。

死時我們同登彼岸，又向不同的世界各奔前程。

This life is the crossing of a sea, where we meet in the same narrow ship.

In death we reach the shore and go to our different worlds.

243

真理的溪流穿過錯誤之河渠而流出。

The stream of truth flows through its channels of
mistakes.

244

今天，我的心因越過那時之海的甜蜜的一點鐘而害思家病。

My heart is homesick to-day for the one sweet hour
across the sea of time.

245

鳥的歌是從大地反響出來的晨光之回聲。

The bird-song is the echo of the morning light back from the earth.

246

「是不是我不值得你來吻我呢？」晨光問杯形花。

"Are you too proud to kiss me?" the morning light asks the buttercup.

247

小花問道：「太陽啊，我要怎樣對你歌唱與崇拜呢？」

太陽回答：「用你純潔的簡單沉默。」

"How may I sing to thee and worship, O Sun?" asked the little flower.

"By the simple silence of thy purity," answered the sun.

248

如果人是畜生，人比畜生更壞。

Man is worse than an animal when he is an animal.

249

當烏雲被光吻著時，便成天上的花朵。

Dark clouds become heaven's flowers when kissed by light.

250

別讓刀鋒譏笑刀柄的厚鈍。

Let not the sword-blade mock its handle for being blunt.

251

夜的靜寂，像一盞深色的燈，是用銀河的光點著的。

The night's silence, like a deep lamp, is burning with the light of its milky way.

252

環繞著生命的晴島，日日夜夜高漲著死亡的海之無窮的歌。

Around the sunny island of Life swells day and night death's limitless song of the sea.

253

是否這座山嶺像一朵花，張開著群峰的花瓣正飲吸著日光呢？

Is not this mountain like a flower, with its petals of hills, drinking the sunlight?

254

把真實的意思讀錯和把他的著重點放錯便成不真實。

The real with its meaning read wrong and emphasis misplaced is the unreal.

255

我的心，從世界的活動中去尋找你的美麗，像帆船的有風與水之優雅。

Find your beauty, my heart, from the world's movement, like the boat that has the grace of the wind and the water.

256

眼睛不拿眼力來傲人，卻以戴眼鏡來傲人。

The eyes are not proud of their sight but of their eyeglasses.

257

我住在我的這個小世界裡，我恐懼著要將這小世界再行縮小。提拔我放進你的世界，讓我有樂於失去我一切的自由。

I live in this little world of mine and am afraid to make it the least less. Lift me into thy world and let me have the freedom gladly to lose my all.

258

虛偽培養在權力中，永遠不能進為真實。

The false can never grow into truth by growing in power.

259

我的心，用歌的輕波，渴想撫愛這晴天的綠色世界。

My heart, with its lapping waves of song, longs to caress this green world of the sunny day.

260

路畔小草，愛著明星吧，於是你的夢想將在花叢中開花
而實現了。

Wayside grass, love the star, then your dreams will
come out in flowers.

261

讓你的音樂像一把利劍，戳進喧鬧市聲的心中去。

Let your music, like a sword, pierce the noise of the
market to its heart.

262

讓樹顫動的葉子像嬰孩的手指般撫觸著我的心。

The trembling leaves of this tree touch my heart like
the fingers of an infant child.

263

我靈魂的憂鬱是她的結婚面紗。

這面紗等著天晚才揭去。

This sadness of my soul is her bride's veil.

It waits to be lifted in the night.

264

這小花躺在塵土裡。

他尋覓那蝴蝶的路徑。

The little flower lies in the dust.

It sought the path of the butterfly.

265

我在路的世界裡。

夜來了。請打開你的大門，你的家之世界。

I am in the world of the roads.

The night comes. Open thy gate, thou world of the home.

266

我已唱完你白天的歌。

在晚上，讓我攜著你的明燈通過那風雨之途。

I have sung the songs of thy day.

In the evening let me carry thy lamp through the stormy path.

267

我不要求你走進這屋裡去。

請到我這無量的荒寂裡來吧，我的愛人。

I do not ask thee into the house.

Come into my infinite loneliness, my Lover.

268

死亡像出生一樣，都是屬於生命的。

走路須要提起腳來，但也須要放下腳去。

Death belongs to life as birth does.

The walk is in the raising of the foot as in the laying of
it down.

269

我已學會你在花叢中和日光下低語的單純意思——教我
知道你在痛苦與死亡中的語句吧。

I have learnt the simple meaning of thy whispers in
flowers and sunshine—teach me to know thy words in
pain and death.

270

這夜之花已經過時,當清晨去吻她,她震顫而嘆息,落
到地上了。

The night's flower was late when the morning kissed
her, she shivered and sighed and dropped to the
ground.

271

透過萬物的憂戚，我聽到「永恆母親」的低唱聲。

Through the sadness of all things I hear the crooning
of the Eternal Mother.

272

大地啊，我來到你的岸邊像一個生人，我住在你的屋中
像一位賓客，我離開你的大門像一位知友。

I came to your shore as a stranger, I lived in your house
as a guest, I leave your door as a friend, my earth.

273

當我去了，讓我的思想到你處來，像那落日的晚霞接連
著星空的靜穆。

Let my thoughts come to you, when I am gone, like the
afterglow of sunset at the margin of starry silence.

274

休息的黃昏，星照耀在我心中，於是讓夜色對我蜜語談愛。

Light in my heart the evening star of rest and then let
the night whisper to me of love.

275

在黑暗中，我是一個小孩。

母親，為了你我伸出兩手透過那黑夜的覆蓋。

I am a child in the dark.

I stretch my hands through the coverlet of night for thee, Mother.

276

白晝的工作做完了，母親，把我的臉埋在你的懷中。

讓我做夢吧。

The day of work is done. Hide my face in your arms, Mother.

Let me dream.

277

會面的燈已點得很久，在分手時，那燈立刻熄了。

The lamp of meeting burns long; it goes out in a moment at the parting.

278

世界啊！當我死了，請給我在你的靜默中保留一句話：「我已愛過了。」

One word keep for me in thy silence, O World, when I am dead, "I have loved."

279

當我們愛這世界時，我們才住在這世界裡。

We live in this world when we love it.

280

讓死的有不朽的名，但活的要有不朽的愛。

Let the dead have the immortality of fame, but the living the immortality of love.

281

我見到你，正如一個半醒的嬰孩在黎明的朦朧中看見他的母親，於是他微笑著又睡去了。

I have seen thee as the half-awakened child sees his mother in the dusk of the dawn and then smiles and sleeps again.

282

我將死了再死的來認識那生命是無盡的。

I shall die again and again to know that life is inexhaustible.

283

當我在路上和眾人一起走過去時，從陽臺上我看見你的微笑，於是我歌唱，於是一切的喧鬧都忘了。

While I was passing with the crowd in the road I saw thy smile from the balcony and I sang and forgot all noise.

284

愛是充實的生命，正如盛滿著酒的杯子一樣。

Love is life in its fulness like the cup with its wine.

285

在他們的廟宇裡，他們點著自己的燈，他們唱著自己的歌。

可是鳥兒卻在你的晨光裡唱著你的名字——因為你的名字就是快樂。

They light their own lamps and sing their own words in their temples.

But the birds sing thy name in thine own morning light,—for thy name is joy.

286

引導我到你的靜默的中心吧，好讓歌聲來充滿我的心。

Lead me in the centre of thy silence to fill my heart
with songs.

287

讓他們住在他們選定的爆竹喧鬧的世界。

我的上帝啊，我的心正渴望著你的星辰。

Let them live who choose in their own hissing world of
fireworks.

My heart longs for thy stars, my God.

288

縈繞我的生命，愛的痛苦唱著，有如深不可測的大海，

愛的歡樂唱著，有如花叢裡的小鳥。

Love's pain sang round my life like the unplumbed sea,

and love's joy sang like birds in its flowering groves.

289

把燈熄了吧，當你深切願望時。

我將知道你的黑暗，我將愛它。

Put out the lamp when thou wishest.

I shall know thy darkness and shall love it.

290

當日子完了我站在你前面，你將看到我的疤痕，明白我曾經受傷，也曾經治癒了。

When I stand before thee at the day's end thou shalt see my scars and know that I had my wounds and also my healing.

291

總有一天在那裡另一個世界的旭光裡，我將對你歌唱：「從前我曾見過你， 在那地球的光中 ， 在那人類的愛裡。」

Some day I shall sing to thee in the sunrise of some other world, "I have seen thee before in the light of the earth, in the love of man."

292

他日的浮雲，飄進我的生命裡，不再滴雨或報風，只為
給我落日的天空染色而來。

Clouds come floating into my life from other days no
longer to shed rain or usher storm but to give colour to
my sunset sky.

293

真理激起反對自己的風暴來便把自己的種子廣播開了。

Truth raises against itself the storm that scatters its
seeds broadcast.

294

昨夜的暴風雨給今晨帶上了黃金的平靜。

The storm of the last night has crowned this morning
with golden peace.

295

真理似乎帶來了終極的話，但終極的話又誕生了下一條
真理。

Truth seems to come with its final word; and the final
word gives birth to its next.

296

名望不超過真實的人是有福的。

Blessed is he whose fame does not outshine his truth.

297

當我忘卻我的名字時，你名字的甜美充滿我心中——像你霧散時的朝陽。

Sweetness of thy name fills my heart when I forget mine—like thy morning sun when the mist is melted.

298

靜寂的夜有慈母的美，喧囂的晝有孩子的美。

The silent night has the beauty of the mother and the clamorous day of the child.

299

當人微笑時世界愛他；當人大笑時世界便怕他了。

The world loved man when he smiled. The world became afraid of him when he laughed.

300

上帝期待著人從智慧裡重獲他的童年。

God waits for man to regain his childhood in wisdom.

301

讓我覺得這世界是你的愛所形成，這樣我的愛可以助它。

Let me feel this world as thy love taking form, then my love will help it.

302

你的陽光含笑地對著我心之冬日，永不疑惑它會開春花。

Thy sunshine smiles upon the winter days of my heart,
never doubting of its spring flowers.

303

上帝的愛只吻著那有限的，人卻吻著無限的。

God kisses the finite in his love and man the infinite.

304

用多年的時日，你渡過空荒年代的沙漠達到那成就的一刻。

Thou crossest desert lands of barren years to reach the
moment of fulfilment.

305

上帝的沉默使人的思想成熟為言論。

God's silence ripens man's thoughts into speech.

306

永恆的旅客啊，在我的歌中你將找到你的足印之形式。

Thou wilt find, Eternal Traveller, marks of thy footsteps across my songs.

307

天父啊，你顯示你的光輝在你的小孩中，讓我不要玷辱你吧。

Let me not shame thee, Father, who displayest thy glory in thy children.

308

這是不快樂的日子，陽光在發怒的雲下像一個受到處罰
小孩在他蒼白的臉上留著淚痕，風的號叫好像一個負創
的世界之呼號。但是我知道我正旅行著去會見我的「朋
友」。

Cheerless is the day, the light under frowning clouds is
like a punished child with traces of tears on its pale
cheeks, and the cry of the wind is like the cry of a
wounded world. But I know I am travelling to meet my
Friend.

309

今夜，在棕櫚樹的葉叢中發生騷動，海裡掀起了波濤，「滿月」，像世界的心之跳動。在你的靜默中，你從什麼未知的天空帶來那愛的痛苦祕密。

To-night there is a stir among the palm leaves, a swell in the sea, Full Moon, like the heart-throb of the world. From what unknown sky hast thou carried in thy silence the aching secret of love?

310

我夢著一顆星——一個光明之島——我就在那裡誕生。
在那有生氣的閒逸深處，我的生命將使我的工作成熟，
有如秋陽下的稻田一般。

I dream of a star, an island of light, where I shall be
born and in the depth of its quickening leisure my life
will ripen its works like the rice-field in the autumn
sun.

311

在雨中溼地的氣味昇起來，有如來自那渺小的群眾的偉
大的無聲讚美歌。

The smell of the wet earth in the rain rises like a great
chant of praise from the voiceless multitude of the
insignificant.

312

那「愛往往會失敗」是我們不能當真理來接受的一種事件。

That love can ever lose is a fact that we cannot accept as
truth.

313

我們終有一天曉得，死亡永不能劫掠我們——劫掠我們
靈魂所獲得的東西，因為靈魂的所獲和靈魂只是一體啊。

We shall know some day that death can never rob us of
that which our soul has gained, for her gains are one
with herself.

314

在我的黃昏的朦朧中上帝到我這裡來，他帶了我過去的
花，這些花在他的花籃中仍保持得很鮮艷。

God comes to me in the dusk of my evening with the
flowers from my past kept fresh in his basket.

315

我主啊，當我生命的絃線全部調和時，於是你的每一撫
觸都會發出愛的音樂來。

When all the strings of my life will be tuned, my
Master, then at every touch of thine will come out the
music of love.

316

上帝啊，讓我真實地活著吧，這樣死亡對我就變成真實了。

Let me live truly, my Lord, so that death to me become true.

317

人的歷史是正在忍耐的等待著那被侮蔑者的凱旋。

Man's history is waiting in patience for the triumph of the insulted man.

318

我覺得此刻你的眼光射在我的心上，有如清晨晴和的靜寂照射收割了的空曠田野。

I feel thy gaze upon my heart this moment like the sunny silence of the morning upon the lonely field whose harvest is over.

319

我渴想著這波濤起伏的那「叫囂之海」彼岸的「歌之島」。

I long for the Island of Songs across this heaving Sea of Shouts.

320

夜的序幕開始於落日的樂曲，這是對不可名狀之黑暗的莊重讚美詩。

The prelude of the night is commenced in the music of the sunset, in its solemn hymn to the ineffable dark.

321

我已攀登那成名的峰巔，發見那裡是一無遮蔽的凜冽而不毛的絕頂。導師啊，請在光線消失以前，領我走進靜寂的山谷，那裡，生命的收穫正成熟為黃金的智慧。

I have scaled the peak and found no shelter in fame's bleak and barren height. Lead me, my Guide, before the light fades, into the valley of quiet where life's harvest mellows into golden wisdom.

322

在薄暮的朦朧中，一切東西看來都像幻影——尖塔的基身消失在黑暗中，而樹頂也像是墨水的汙斑。我將等待著清晨，我將醒來看見你的城市在光之中。

Things look phantastic in this dimness of the dusk— the spires whose bases are lost in the dark and tree-tops like blots of ink. I shall wait for the morning and wake up to see thy city in the light.

323

我曾經受苦，我曾經失望，而且我懂得什麼是死，於是我很樂意於我在這偉大的世界。

I have suffered and despaired and known death and I am glad that I am in this great world.

324

在我的生命中有些地方是空白的是閒靜的。這些地方都是空曠之區，我忙碌的日子便在那裡得到了陽光與空氣。

There are tracts in my life that are bare and silent. They are the open spaces where my busy days had their light and air.

325

解救我吧，我的不滿足的過去從後面緊抱著我不容我死，請來解救我吧。

Release me from my unfulfilled past clinging to me from behind making death difficult.

326

讓這做我的最後一句話吧，「我信賴你的愛。」

Let this be my last word, that I trust in thy love.

譯者附註

查悉泰翁《漂鳥集》中詩，大多係直接用英文撰寫，拙譯根據單行本，其中九十八首與二六三首相同，為重複，而在《泰戈爾詩歌戲劇合集》中，已將二六三首刪去，以二六四首改作二六三首，以下各首均依現遞前，成三二五首版本，本書仍照舊本，特加說明。

泰戈爾小說戲劇集

糜文開 裴普賢 譯

階級、宗教與國家，誰能帶來終極正義？

這把「戀之火」若燒得過國族與宗教的藩籬，能否看到「奚德蘿」的永恆真我？還是剩下「骷髏」般的寡婦軀體，為受莫名的歧視，而暗自泣血？

在道德與自我之間，誰來成全我們的愛情？

心愛的人就在眼前，是什麼阻止我伸手擁抱？就讓時間駐留在這「無上的一夜」吧！

印度文學欣賞 (二版)

糜文開 著

印度文化以宗教為核心，印度歷史就等於一部宗教的演變史，而印度文學史也就可依宗教的演變來分期。婆羅門教、佛教、印度教、回教、基督宗教，分別引導過印度的發展，也分別發展出各具特色的詩歌、寓言、戲劇、小說作品。曾經通行過的語言如梵文、巴利文、波斯文、興地文、烏都文，也因多變的聲韻幻化出綺麗豐富的風情。本書選譯了印度歷史上的代表作，如婆羅門時期：吠陀經、奧義書；佛教時期：《佛所行讚》、《大莊嚴經》、《百喻經》；印度教時期：《五卷書》、《四部箴》；以及近代大文豪：泰戈爾、奈都莎綠琴尼、普雷姜德的作品。敬邀讀者大眾一同欣賞印度文學多樣的風貌！

印度文學歷代名著選 (上)(下)

糜文開 編譯

本書係糜教授繼《印度文學欣賞》的精心編譯，是當今印度文學的唯一讀本。內容先將印度文學史分成五期敘述，介紹各期的名著及其作者，於是選錄作品，偏重文學趣味，上自吠佛讚歌，下迄印度獨立後的國歌及方言作品，共約四百篇，六十餘萬字。

新月集

泰戈爾 著／糜文開 糜榴麗 譯

《新月集》為印度詩哲泰戈爾的童詩集，於 1913 年出版，略早於《漂鳥集》，但在中文世界的讚譽不亞於之。泰戈爾的童詩純樸真摯，有兒童的異想天開，亦有母親的滿腔溫情。《新月集》簡單的文字充滿童趣，同時承載著深刻的情感，彷彿新月般的溫暖臂彎，能喚醒一顆顆無憂無慮的、童稚的心。